Joseph and His Brothers
And Other Bible Stories

BY REBECCA GLASER

ILLUSTRATED BY BILL FERENC AND EMMA TRITHART

SPARK
HOUSE
FAMILY

MINNEAPOLIS

Contents

24 23 22 21 20 19 18 17 16 15   1 2 3 4 5 6 7 8
ISBN: 978-1-4514-9995-7

Book design by Toolbox Studios, Dave Wheeler, Alisha Lofgren, and Janelle Markgren
Illustrations by Bill Ferenc and Emma Trithart

Library of Congress Cataloging-in-Publication Data

Glaser, Rebecca Stromstad, author.
  Joseph and his brothers and other Bible stories / by Rebecca Glaser ; illustrated by Bill Ferenc and Emma Trithart.
        pages cm. — (Holy Moly Bible storybooks)
  Summary: «Illustrated retellings of the story of Joseph and His Brothers and other favorite Bible stories."— Provided by publisher.
  Audience: Ages 5–8
  Audience: K to grade 3
  ISBN 978-1-4514-9995-7 (alk. paper)
1. Joseph (Son of Jacob)—Juvenile literature. 2. Jacob (Biblical patriarch)—Juvenile literature. 3. Bible stories, English—Genesis. I. Ferenc, Bill, illustrator. II. Trithart, Emma, illustrator. III. Title.
  BS580.J6G53 2015
  222.1109505—dc23
                        2015012805
Printed on acid-free paper

Printed in U.S.A.

V63474; 9781451499957; AUG2015

Jacob and Esau

Isaac and Rebekah had twin boys named Esau and Jacob. The brothers fought a lot, even before they were born! Esau was born first, and Jacob came next holding on to Esau's heel.

The brothers were very different. Hairy Esau loved to hunt. Smooth-skinned Jacob liked to stay by the tents. Esau was Isaac's favorite, but Rebekah loved Jacob most. Because Esau was the oldest, he would someday receive his father's blessing for the firstborn.

One day, Esau was very hungry.
He asked Jacob for stew.
"First let me have your blessing,"
Jacob said.

"Okay, you can be number one,"
Esau said. "Just let me eat!"

When Isaac was very old and couldn't see, he told Esau it was time to give his blessing. Rebekah overheard and rushed to Jacob. "Psst," Rebekah whispered. "It's time to take your father's blessing."

While Esau was hunting, Jacob put on Esau's clothes. He covered his arms in hairy goatskin and went to his father.

"Who's there?" Isaac asked.
"It's Esau," Jacob lied.
Isaac felt Jacob's hairy arms and smelled him. The disguise worked! Isaac gave Jacob his blessing. Now Jacob was number one!

Color in Jacob as he's being blessed.

Esau was furious with Jacob! Afraid, Jacob ran far away from home.

Jacob Becomes Israel

Jacob set up camp along a river. It had been many years since he stole Esau's blessing. Finally, he was on his way home.

It was dark and quiet, and Jacob was alone.
Suddenly a man appeared and grabbed him.
Left, right, up, down! Punch, kick, grapple, fight!
Jacob wrestled the mysterious man ALL night.

Just when the sun was peeking over the horizon,
the man knocked Jacob's hip out of its socket.
"Let me go!" the man demanded.
"First, give me a blessing." Jacob said.
"What's your name?" the man asked.
"Jacob," he replied.
"I will give you a new name," the man said.
"You will be called Israel because you have
struggled with God and won."
Then God blessed Jacob.

Joseph and His Brothers

1, 2, 3, 4, 5, 6, 7, 8, 9, 10, 11, 12!
Jacob had twelve sons. But he
had one favorite—Joseph.
Jacob gave Joseph a big, beautiful robe.
The eleven other brothers
were jealous!

One night Joseph dreamed tha[t] stars and grain bowed to him. He realized that someday, his family would bow down to him the same way the stars and grain did. Joseph's dream made his brothers angry!

Joseph's brothers went to tend sheep far away from home. Jacob sent Joseph out to check on them.

Draw a picture of a dream you've had.

Joseph's angry brothers plotted to get rid of him. When they saw him coming, they grabbed Joseph and tore off his fancy robe.

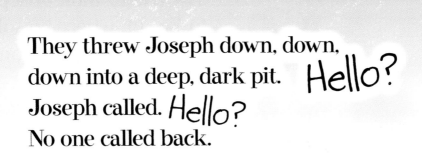

They threw Joseph down, down, down into a deep, dark pit. Hello? Joseph called. Hello? No one called back.

Just then, a trader passed by. Not wanting to kill Joseph, the brothers decided to sell him to the trader. "Then we'll be rid of him for good," they said.

The trader took Joseph to Egypt, where he sold Joseph to work for one of Pharaoh's officers.

Joseph Interprets Pharaoh's Dream

Pharaoh, the ruler of Egypt, was worried about his dreams. In one dream, seven thin cows ate seven plump ones. In another, seven dying stalks of grain swallowed up seven healthy ones. Pharaoh wondered . . .

"WHAT do these dreams MEAN?"

Pharaoh called
all his wise men and
magicians together. "Please,
tell me what my dreams mean!"
Pharaoh pleaded.
But nobody knew.

Color in Pharaoh's dream.

20

Then one of Pharaoh's servants had an idea. "I know a man who can tell you what your dreams mean!" he said.

The servant rushed to get Joseph and bring him to Pharaoh. Joseph was worried! What did Pharaoh want?

"Tell me what my dreams mean!" Pharaoh demanded.

Relieved, Joseph nodded and said, "The meaning of your dreams won't come from me but from God. Egypt will have seven years of food galore. But then, there will be seven years of no food at all. Store up food during the years of plenty, and eat it during the years of famine."

Pharaoh was astounded! He made Joseph a great ruler in Egypt and put him in charge of storing food. For seven years, they collected food to store. So when there was no more food to gather, they still had enough to eat!

Joseph Forgives

Famine spread far and wide across the land outside Egypt. Crops couldn't grow. There wasn't anything to eat. People traveled from all over to buy food from Egypt.

Far away, Joseph's family was running out of food. Jacob sent his sons to buy grain in Egypt. They didn't know their brother Joseph was a great ruler there who controlled all the food supplies!

When the brothers came to ask for food,
Joseph recognized them right away.
The brothers bowed down to Joseph,
just like in his dreams from long ago.

Joseph jumped up and exclaimed,
"It's me, your lost brother!
Is our father still alive?
Bring him here too!"

Joseph's brothers were amazed and shocked! They raced to bring Jacob to Egypt. Jacob couldn't wait to see his favorite son again!

Joseph rushed to give his father a big hug. "I missed you so much!" he cried. Filled with joy, Jacob embraced his son. Father, son, and the eleven brothers were finally reunited.

More Activities

LOOK AND FIND

Find the

in the Jacob and Esau story on page 3.

The name Jacob means "heel-grabber."

Find the

in the Jacob Becomes Israel story on page 9.

The name Israel means "one who strives with God."

Find the  in the Joseph and His Brothers story on page 13.

Jacob only gave one of his twelve sons a colorful coat.

Find the

in the Joseph Interprets Pharaoh's Dream story on pages 19-24.

The servant who told Pharaoh about Joseph was called the "chief cupbearer" or butler.

Find the

in the Joseph Forgives story on page 25.

Joseph's brothers traveled from the land of Canaan to Egypt to find food.

ACTION PRAYER

Dear God,

You were with Joseph and his family when they were happy. *(make a happy face)*

You were with Joseph and his family when they were sad. *(make a sad face)*

You were with Joseph and his family when they were angry. *(make an angry face)*

You were with Joseph and his family when they were scared. *(make a scared face)*

You were with Joseph and his family when they were at peace.
(make a peaceful face)

You are always with us, no matter what we are feeling.

Today I am feeling . . . *(share your word, and make a face to show that feeling).*

Amen.

MATCHING GAME

Match the person from the Bible with the fact about them.

1. I was born first, but my twin brother tricked our father and stole my blessing and birthright.

2. I ruled over Egypt. My title means "king."

3. Our names are: Reuben, Simeon, Levi, Judah, Issachar, Zebulun, Dan, Naphtali, Gad, Asher, and Benjamin.

4. My jealous and angry brothers were unkind to me. I still loved them, forgave them, and fed them.

5. God changed my name. My twelve sons represented the twelve tribes of Israel.

6. I first met Joseph in prison, where Joseph told me about my dreams.

1. Esau; 2. Pharaoh; 3. Joseph's brothers; 4. Joseph; 5. Jacob; 6. Chief cupbearer